Night Lights

A Sukkot Story

By Barbara Diamond Goldin · Illustrated by Amberin Huq

 PJ Library®

With love to my brother, Robert,
and his family, Diana, Rachel, and Ferris
— BDG

For Mum and Dad
— AH

Apples & Honey Press
An imprint of Behrman House Publishers
Millburn, New Jersey 07041
www.applesandhoneypress.com

Text copyright © 2020 by Barbara Diamond Goldin
Illustrations copyright © 2020 by Amberin Huq

Text adapted from Night Lights: A Sukkot Story
copyright © 1995, 2002 by Barbara Diamond Goldin

ISBN 978-1-68115-5470

Library of Congress Cataloging-in-Publication Data

Names: Goldin, Barbara Diamond, author. | Huq, Amberin, illustrator.
Title: Night lights : a Sukkot story / by Barbara Diamond Goldin ;
illustrated by Amberin Huq.
Description: Millburn, New Jersey : Apples & Honey Press, an imprint of
Behrman House, [2020] | Summary: A young boy learns about the
meaning of Sukkot while overcoming his fear of the dark.
Identifiers: LCCN 2019024920 | ISBN 9781681155470 (hardcover)
Subjects: CYAC: Sukkot—Fiction. | Fear of the dark—Fiction.
| Jews—United States—Fiction.
Classification: LCC PZ7.G5674 Ni 2020 | DDC [E]—dc23
LC record available at https://lccn.loc.gov/2019024920

Design by Elynn Cohen
Edited by Dena Neusner
Art Directed by Ann D. Koffsky
Printed in Turkey

The illustrations were drawn and painted digitally using a variety of brushes and textures.

1 3 5 7 9 8 6 4 2

Customization code: 092031K2/B556/A5

"Can't we put a real roof on it? Just this once?" Daniel pleaded, as his dad and mom nailed the boards together for the sukkah, the little hut the family put up each year for the holiday of Sukkot.

"No roof," said Dad. "Just branches. A sukkah isn't a house."

"And we're supposed to see the sky through the roof," Daniel's big sister, Naomi, chimed in. She was in religious school and liked to show off.

"That way we remember our ancestors who left Egypt thousands of years ago."

"That's right," said Mom. "They had to sleep in huts
like this one when they stopped at night in the desert."
"They must have been very brave," said Daniel.

"Don't worry," said Naomi, as she tied apples to the branches with string so they dangled in the air. "It'll be fun to sleep in the sukkah tonight. And we'll be all by ourselves this year, since Grandpa has a cold."

"I loved sleeping in the sukkah when I was a little girl," added Mom.

Daniel wasn't so sure.

He thought of the holes in the roof and the scary noises at night, like the ones they'd heard last year. Could a bear climb up there? Or a wolf?

He shivered as he piled fat squash, yellow and orange and green squash, lumpy and crooked squash on the table.

"We're done!" said Dad.
"You're such good helpers."

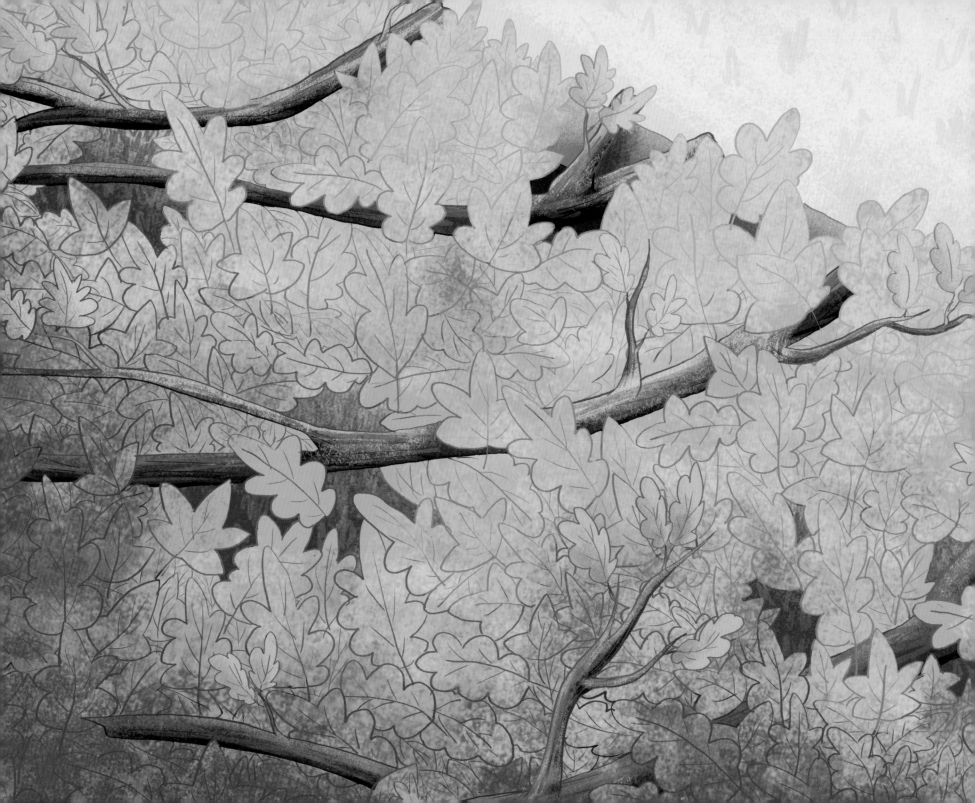

Daniel and Naomi stood looking at the little sukkah after Dad and Mom went inside to make dinner. "It's so colorful," said Naomi. "The decorations are even better than last year's."

Daniel didn't say a word.

"Don't tell me you're too scared to sleep in it," Naomi said.

"I slept in it last year, didn't I?"

Naomi snickered. "Yes, with Grandpa singing you to sleep."

"I'm not afraid of the dark anymore," Daniel said. "Not since Mama bought me a night light."

"You can't have your night light in a sukkah," Naomi said. "There's no plug. Do you think our ancestors had night lights when they lived in their *sukkot*?"

"Maybe," said Daniel.

"Thousands of years ago? You must be kidding. All they had was the desert sand and rocks and whatever they brought from Egypt. Besides, you'll be scared at the first noise." She made a growly face at Daniel.

"I will not," said Daniel.

"Time for supper," Dad called from the house. "Come and help carry all this food outside."

Everyone ate in the sukkah that evening. The neighbors came too. They had to wear sweaters, and their chairs bumped against each other, but the air was crisp and cool, and the food tasted extra good.

The sound of their talk and laughter bounced all around them, off the walls and up through the branches, into the night sky.

Maybe it won't be so bad sleeping in the sukkah, Daniel thought.

After dinner, Daniel helped bring the dishes back into the house. Soon the sukkah was empty again, of people and food, sounds and light.

Naomi and Daniel carried their blankets and pillows outside and put them in the corner of the sukkah. Daniel had his teddy bear too.

"Are you sure you want to sleep out here?" he whispered. Teddy didn't answer.

Daniel settled down next to Naomi, twisting and turning in his blanket bed on the ground.

"I can't go to sleep with all your squirming," complained Naomi. Daniel closed his eyes and tried to lie still.

It wasn't quiet for long.

Whooo.

The wind started up. It blew through the branches and shook the walls.

"It's just the wind," whispered Naomi.

"Why are you whispering?" asked Daniel. "Are you scared too?"

"Of course not," she said. But her voice squeaked a little.

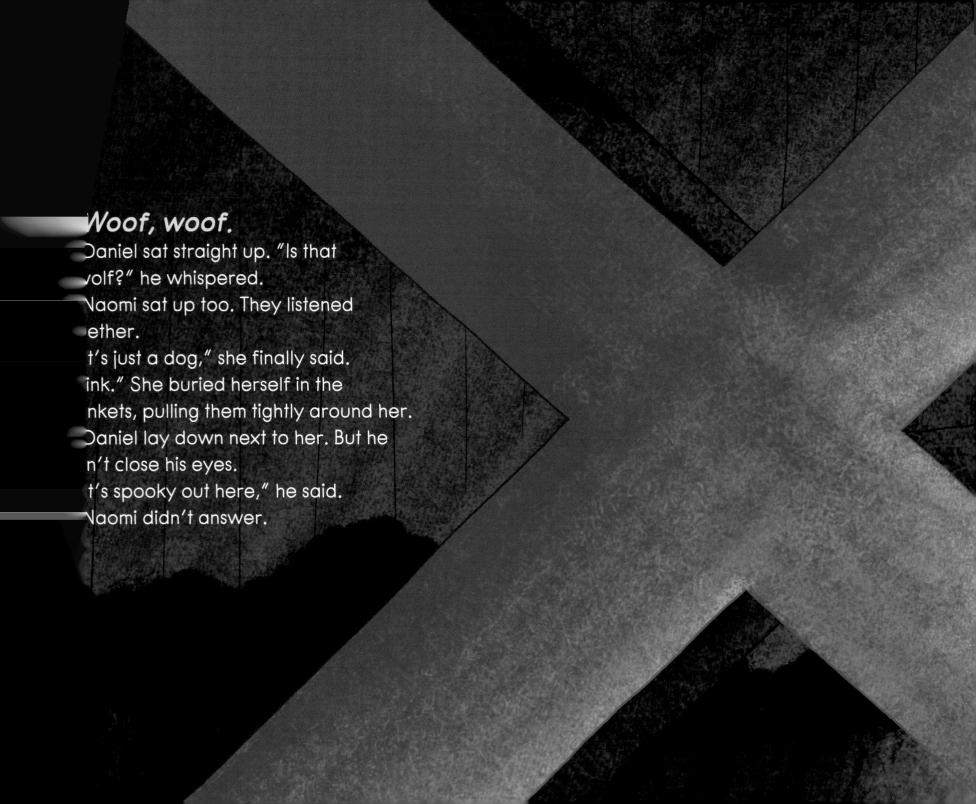

Woof, woof.

Daniel sat straight up. "Is that
wolf?" he whispered.

Naomi sat up too. They listened
ether.

t's just a dog," she finally said.

ink." She buried herself in the
nkets, pulling them tightly around her.

Daniel lay down next to her. But he
n't close his eyes.

t's spooky out here," he said.

Naomi didn't answer.

Daniel lay awake, his eyes searching every corner of the hut.

He began to see faces where the squash were supposed to be. Mean, lumpy, grinning faces.

He stood up, clutching his bear.
It was too hard being an ancestor.

Just then, Naomi put out her hand and tugged at Daniel.

"Don't go. Please," she said softly. "Keep me company."

"I'm too scared," he said. "Aren't you?"

"A little," Naomi admitted. She was quiet, staring at the sky through the branches.

"You know, Daniel, maybe our ancestors did have night lights in the desert."

"But you said there were no plugs. . . ."
"I know, I know. But . . ." She held up Daniel's covers.
"Slide in here and look up."

Daniel snuggled inside his blanket and looked up. Through the branches he saw bright stars and a gigantic moon. "Night lights," answered Daniel. "Lots of them! And the moon too!" He smiled at all the sparkling lights. He'd never noticed how many there were. The sky was full of them.

"Our ancestors had the first night lights," said Naomi.

Daniel felt warm and cozy now, next to Naomi. Maybe our ancestors were brave, and a little scared, too, like me, he thought.

So, like the ancestors in the desert, Daniel and Naomi watched the night lights above them.

And soon they fell asleep.

Sukkot, the Festival of Booths, is a weeklong fall holiday. To celebrate Sukkot, Jews all over the world build huts, or *sukkot*, with leafy branches for roofs. Sukkot commemorates the forty years that the Israelites wandered in the desert after the Exodus from Egypt and lived in temporary shelters.

Building a sukkah also reminds us that our ancestors became farmers in the Promised Land and built temporary huts near their crops at harvest time.

A sukkah isn't a house, as Dad tells Daniel in the story. It has holes in the roof and doesn't provide much protection from the rain, cold, or wind. Being in a sukkah reminds us of how vulnerable we are when it comes to the forces of nature and how dependent we are on the natural world.

Just as Daniel felt afraid to sleep in the sukkah, our ancestors might have felt afraid in their *sukkot*. People today who live in temporary shelters, such as refugees from war-torn countries, probably feel more afraid than they would in their own homes. Sukkot gives us a chance to see and feel what it's like to live in a temporary home.

Although he was afraid, Daniel was able to find comfort in the sukkah, by looking at the moon and the stars. Have you ever been somewhere you felt afraid? What helped you to feel safe?

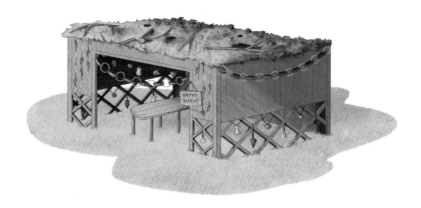